This book belongs to:

......Jess..........

....

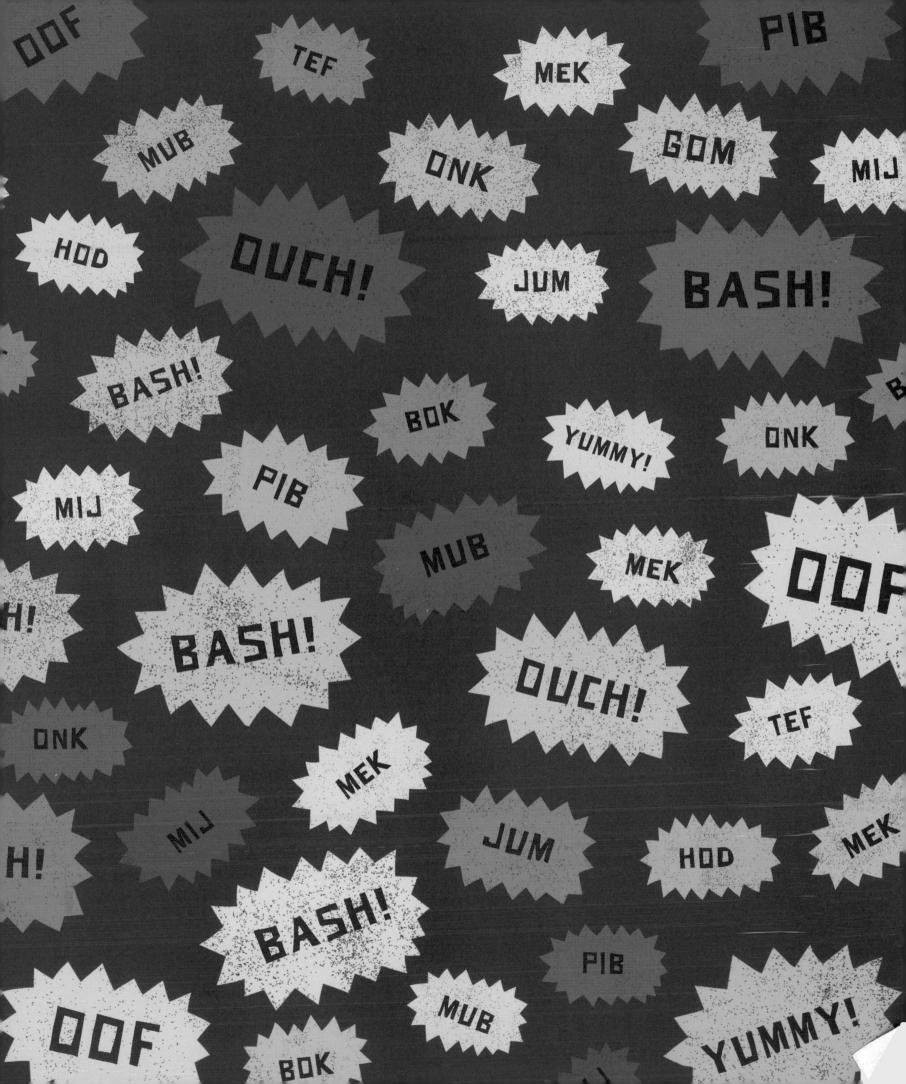

For Alison & Genevieve

A TEMPLAR BOOK

First published in the UK in 2020 by Templar Books,
an imprint of Bonnier Books UK,
The Plaza, 535 King's Road, London, SW10 0SZ
www.templarco.co.uk
www.bonnierbooks.co.uk

Text and ilustrations copyright © 2020 by Duncan Beedie
Design copyright © 2020 by Templar Books

1 3 5 7 9 10 8 6 4 2

ISBN 978-1-78741-681-9
This book was typeset in Clarendon
The illustrations were created digitally

Designed by Genevieve Webster
Edited by Alison Ritchie
Printed in China

OOF MAKES AN

OUCH!

DUNCAN BEEDIE

templar
books

Many, many years ago, before your
great-great-great-great-great grandparents
were born (and before their grandparents,
for that matter!), there was a little girl
called Oof.

Oof's best friend was a little boy called Pib.

Oof and Pib did everything together.

They lived in an ancient village
where no one knew any words apart
from their own name.

Oof would call out
every day.

PIB!

Pib would reply.

It made conversation a bit tricky,
but they managed to get by, whether they were
playing together, exploring together . . .

. . . or inventing things together.

Oof and Pib were **inseparable.**

One day, Oof and Pib were thinking
of new inventions, when Oof had
a **brilliant** idea!

Hod!

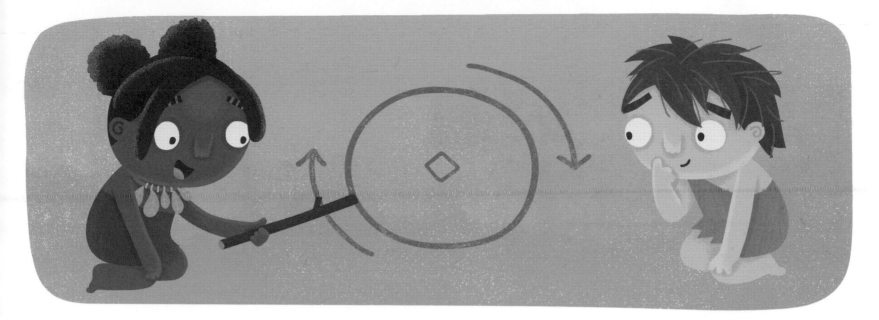

"Oof! Oof!" she cried out excitedly and drew a picture of it in the sand.

O-O-O-O-F!

P-I-I-I-B!

What they needed was the perfect rock, but the one they found was **very** heavy.

When they tried to lift it, it slipped from their hands and landed right on Oof's foot!

Poor Oof.

It really hurt – but she couldn't express just how much, until . . .

The grown-ups stopped what they were doing and stared.
"Onk?" enquired Onk.
"Tef?" exclaimed Tef.
"Mij!" said Mij, and "Jum!" cried Jum.

They couldn't believe it.
Oof had invented a **new word** . . .

And they couldn't wait to try it out!

Oof's foot was feeling a bit better, but she was still angry at the silly rock. As she swung her club at it, she shouted yet **another** new word.

"BAAASSHH!" the others yelled as they joined in.

(If the rock could talk it almost certainly would have said "ouch!".)

All that excitement
had made everyone hungry.
And as Oof bit into the
sweet, juicy berries, *another*
new word came to her.

Yummy!

Yummy!

Yummy!

"Yummy!" the villagers chimed together.

Oof was a hero!
And as the villagers helped to carry the rock
to her hut, they chanted the new words
in celebration.

That afternoon, Oof took a sharp piece of stone
and began chipping away at the rock.

But Oof was much
too busy, so Pib played
on his own . . .

and explored
on his own . . .

and then he
skulked back to his
hut on his own.

As night fell, Oof covered up
her newly-finished creation, ready for its
grand unveiling the next day.

Pib lay in his hut next door.
He couldn't sleep. He felt angry . . . more than angry.
The grown-ups thought Oof was a genius,
and it made Pib jealous.

But, unlike Oof, he couldn't invent any words to express
his feelings . . . which made him even angrier.

So Pib picked up his club and went out to find
something to BASH instead.

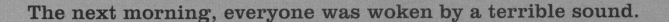
The next morning, everyone was woken by a terrible sound.

All of Oof's hard work
had been ruined.

Pib felt awful. He never meant to upset his friend.
He wanted a new word to tell her how he felt,
to try and make things better . . . but he couldn't speak.

He felt like he had a stone lodged in his throat.

Then, he felt something rising up from his tummy,
and into his mouth, until it finally came out . . .

Oof was **stunned.**
She had never heard this word before,
but somehow she knew *exactly*
what it meant.

"Oof sorry," she said back.

The two friends hugged.

Then Pib had a **brilliant** idea.

He ran into the forest and came back with some strong vines.

After a lot of grunting and puffing, the invention was mended.
And so was Oof and Pib's friendship.

The grown-ups looked on in **amazement** at Oof and Pib's creation.
They were pretty sure it would be **very** useful.

If they could only figure out how . . .

As for Oof and Pib –
they knew **exactly** what to do with it.

Also by Duncan Beedie:

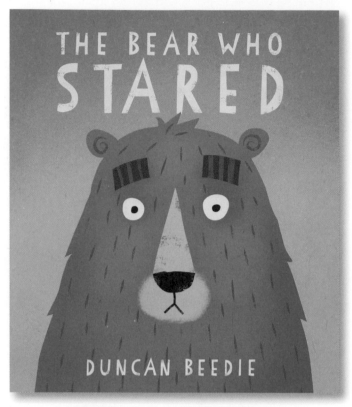

ISBN: 978-1-78370-375-3

ISBN: 978-1-78741-340-5

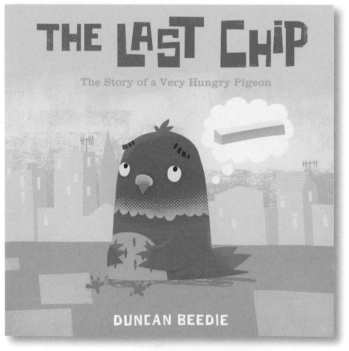

ISBN: 978-1-78370-062-2

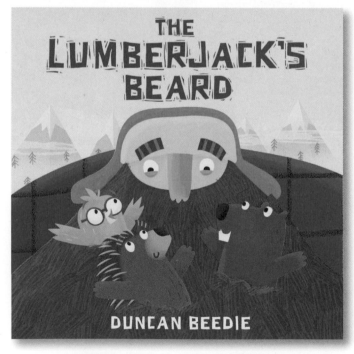

ISBN: 978-1-78370-688-4